OLD BIRD

To the real Old Bird, and to her owner, Archie, who grew up to be my dad
— I.M.

For my grandson Colin, with much love and gratitude
— M.W.

_____

Text copyright © 2003 by Irene Morck
Illustrations copyright © 2003 by Muriel Wood

Published in Canada by Fitzhenry & Whiteside, 195 Allstate Parkway, Markham, Ontario L3R 4T8

Published in the United States by Fitzhenry & Whiteside, 121 Harvard Avenue, Suite 2, Allston, Massachusetts 02134

www.fitzhenry.ca   godwit@fitzhenry.ca

10 9 8 7 6 5 4 3 2 1

Morck, Irene
Old bird / by Irene Morck ; illustrations by Muriel Wood.

ISBN 1-55041-695-2 (bound).—ISBN 1-55041-697-9 (pbk.)

1. Horses—Juvenile fiction. I. Wood, Muriel II. Title.

PS8576.O628O43 2002   jC813'.54   C2002-901608-8
PZ7

U.S. Publisher Cataloging-in-Publication Data
(Library of Congress Standards)

Morck, Irene.
Old bird / by Irene Morck ; illustrated by Muriel Wood.—1st ed.
[32] p. : col. ill. ;   cm.
Summary: Father buys an old mare to carry Archie and his brother to school every day.
But the stubborn old horse has other ideas about her place on the farm. And in the battle of wills that follows,
Bird gets a chance to show that she's not ready to go out to pasture just yet.
ISBN 1-55041-695-2
ISBN 1-55041-697-9 (pbk.)
1. Horses — Fiction — Juvenile literature. [Horses — Fiction.] I. Wood, Muriel. II. Title.
[E] 21 2002   AC CIP

Fitzhenry & Whiteside acknowledges with thanks the Canada Council for the Arts, the Government of Canada through the
Book Publishing Industry Development Program (BPIDP), and the Ontario Arts Council for their support for our publishing program.

Design by Wycliffe Smith Design
Printed in Hong Kong

OLD BIRD

➤ I R E N E M O R C K • M U R I E L W O O D ❬

F i t z h e n r y & W h i t e s i d e

Today was Arnfeld's first day of school. He knew it would take forever to walk from the homestead to the schoolhouse. Four miles along the wagon trail. Four miles back.

Archie had to get used to waiting for his little brother now. Arnfeld's legs were dragging—slower, slower. Two whole hours there. Two whole hours back.

Papa was in the field plowing when Archie and Arnfeld trudged into the yard. Their chores were still waiting. They had to haul water. Bring in firewood. Feed the pigs. Feed the chickens. Gather the eggs. Shovel out the barn. Put down clean straw. Even with Mama's help, it was slow going.

That evening, supper was late. The rest of the week proved no better.

On Saturday Mama announced, "Papa's gone to an auction to buy another workhorse." The boys nodded. It took lots of power to clear the forest and break homestead land for grain. They needed a third workhorse.

But instead Papa brought back a little, old mare.

"I couldn't afford any of the workhorses," he said. "All I could get was this old thing. But at least you boys can ride to school now. You can get your chores done and we can eat on time. Her name is Bird."

"Bird?" whispered Arnfeld. "Bird. You're pretty."

"Oh, Papa. Thank you, thank you," Archie said, turning his face away, hugging the mare's silky neck.

All that afternoon, Bird followed Archie and Arnfeld. Even when the boys cleaned out the chicken coop, the old horse walked back and forth with them as they dumped load after load of manure.

But sometimes Bird would stop by the fence to stare across the field where Papa and the team were plowing the earth—slowly, slowly.

That evening a storm blew in. When Papa, Archie, and Arnfeld headed out to milk the cows, Bird followed them to the barn.

"Sorry, Old Bird," Papa said. "No room for horses. Five cows, five stalls." He shut the door and turned the wooden latch.

A moment later the door opened, letting in the howling wind and cold rain. Bird stepped into the barn.

"She must have just rubbed the latch with her nose," said Papa. He chased the old horse outside and closed the door firmly.

In no time Bird was back inside. Papa chased her out.

Bird opened the door again. Papa grumbled and shook his head. But Bird didn't leave the barn until Papa and the boys were finished milking.

In the morning Papa showed the boys the new latch he'd made.

He laughed. "Old Bird, you can't open this one."

They had hardly sat down to milk when the door swung open. Bird strolled into the barn.

"That's strange," said Papa. "She must have been chewing on the rope. Just happened to pull on the part that opens it." He chased her out and locked the door. Almost immediately, Bird was back in the barn.

"No!" cried Papa. He threw his milk stool. The stool bounced off Bird's shoulder and she scrambled out. Papa locked the door, grabbed his stool and went back to work.

Bird opened the latch and peeked in the doorway.

"Impossible!" Papa exploded. This time, Bird calmly stepped aside, watched the milk stool go flying past, and then sauntered into the barn. Muttering, Papa tramped into the rain to retrieve his stool.

On Monday Bird carried Archie and Arnfeld to school. She obeyed every command. In the schoolyard the children gathered around to admire the new horse. And when the boys returned home that afternoon, Mama and Papa were beaming.

"You're back so soon," said Papa.

"In plenty of time for chores," said Mama. "And guess what. Your papa has come up with a brand new latch. I couldn't open it until he showed me how."

"Now, step back," said Papa. "Let's see how soon Old Bird gives up on this one."

But Bird used her teeth just as Papa used his hands. In seconds she had the latch open.

The next day, Papa made a different latch. Bird opened that one too.

"I'll outsmart you yet," growled Papa.

Finally on Wednesday morning, Papa had created a latch that Bird could not open. They milked the cows in peace.

Papa chuckled. "Got you, Old Bird."

That very morning on the way to school, Bird lifted her back legs ever so gently. Arnfeld slid off one side, pulling Archie down with him.

"Something must have scared her," said Archie.

On the way home, it happened again. Bird stopped in a mud puddle, lowered her head, and bucked gently. The boys lay in the gooey muck.

"What happened?" asked Mama when they reached home.

"She bucked us off," Archie answered.

Mama frowned. "Bird? Impossible." Bird stood quietly, staring across the field where Papa and the team were plowing. "She's a sweet old horse," added Mama. "You boys were fooling around. You have to be more careful."

The next day Bird bucked more often. They were late for school and late getting home.

"That horse really does buck," said Mama as they rode into the yard, covered with fresh grass stains. "We can't keep a horse that doesn't behave."

"But she just started it yesterday," said Archie. "And she doesn't buck hard."

"It's like riding a toboggan," Arnfeld said. "Fun if you stay on. Just as much fun if you fall off."

Archie nodded. "And she'll teach us to be good riders."

Mama looked sad. "It takes a lot of scrubbing to get out mud and grass stains," she said.

Bird stood quietly, staring across the field.

Friday, on the way to school, Bird dumped them into a bush. Archie's shirt was torn. When the boys headed home that afternoon, Archie had a note from the teacher tucked into his pants pocket.

Papa frowned as he read the note. "The teacher says that you were late for school again. And she is worried that you're going to get hurt when you fall off." He folded the note. "We can't afford to feed a horse that is making things worse, not better."

Mama looked glum. "I can't be scrubbing and patching every day."

"There's an auction tomorrow afternoon," said Papa.

"No, Papa! No!" cried the boys. "Please."

Papa just shook his head.

The next morning, Bird stood at the fence while the boys went with Papa to help hook the team to the plow. Just as the team started, Old Bird let out a frantic whinny.

Then she jumped right over the fence.

Bird galloped to the big horses and lined up beside them. Digging her hooves into the heavy earth, neck arched and muscles straining, Bird plodded alongside the team.

"Get a halter," said Papa. "Tie up this crazy horse. This afternoon, she's going to the auction."

Arnfeld and Archie ran to the barn. But instead of the halter, they dragged back the extra harness.

"Bird wants to plow," Arnfeld said.

Papa shook his head. "Impossible. She's too little for plowing."

"Please, Papa," said Archie. "It won't hurt to try her."

Papa sighed. "Well, I guess you won't believe me unless you see for yourselves." He flung the harness on Bird and adjusted it. Bird bent her head low, so Archie could slip the bit into her mouth and slide the bridle over her ears. Then the boys helped Papa hook Bird to the plow.

"Well, Old Bird, let's see if you can keep up." Papa grinned. "Gid-up."

Bird leaned into the harness. Before the big horses had even tightened their traces, the plow moved forward. And as the other horses shouldered the weight, Bird kept pulling. Her muscles bulged. Her hooves dug deep into the dirt. Papa steered the plow, his eyes wide.

Around and around the field, the plow sliced through the dry grass, making ridges of fresh, black soil. Bird pulled as hard as the big horses. The plow moved faster than ever before.

"Never seen anything like it," said Papa. "She sure can work," he added, shaking his head.

That evening, when they were milking the cows, Papa said, "I guess it must be lonely outside." He unlocked the door and held it open.

Old Bird ambled into the barn.

On Monday the boys rode to school and back in record time.

"No bucking at all," said Arnfeld sadly.

Archie smiled. "No grass stains, no mud, no torn clothes."

"Never seen anything like it," said Papa.

No one spoke again about selling Old Bird. Every day Bird carried the boys to school and back. No bucking at all. Every afternoon, she worked in the field with the team.

And at milking time, Papa would open the barn door and wait for Old Bird.

Then he would close the door behind them.